The Didgeridu Crew

Written and illustrated by
Anne Kerr

Published by Boolarong Press,
655 Toohey Road
Salisbury Qld 4107
Australia.
www.boolarongpress.com.au

First published 2017

Cataloguing-in-Publication entry available at the National Library of Australia

Creator: Kerr, Anne Maxine, author.

Title: The didgeridu crew / Anne Kerr.

ISBN: 9781925522020 (paperback)

Target Audience: For primary school age.

Subjects: Children–Juvenile fiction.
Didgeridu–Juvenile fiction.
Crocodiles–Juvenile fiction.
Adventure stories.

Dewey Number: A823.4

Printed and bound by Watson Ferguson & Company, Salisbury, Australia

Three cheers to friendship, adventure
and knowing when to run!

Out in the bush far away from the busy cities and towns lived three adventurous boys. The first boy was Tom. The second boy was Tim. The third boy was Gavin.

Tom had a spear.
He had made it himself.

When he threw it, the spear went

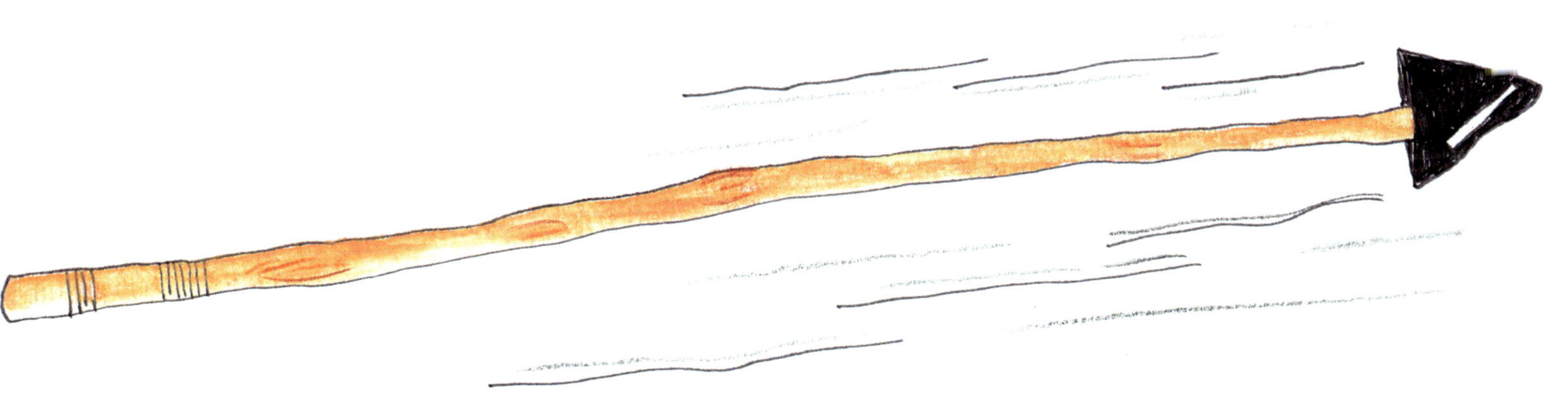

Tim had an axe which his dad had helped him make.

When he used it, the axe went

Chop!
Chop!

Gavin had a boomerang. His grandfather had given it to him a long time ago. It was very special to him.

When he threw it into the air,
the boomerang went

Tom, Tim and Gavin each had their own didgeridoo.

When they blew into them the didgeridoos made a wonderful WOOM WOOMMA WOOM WOOMMA sound!

The three boys were mates and would often go down to the billabong near their homes for a cool swim. Wherever they went they always took their amazing 'toys' with them.

BEWARE
CROCS!

At the billabong, the three adventurous boys had to be on the lookout for crocodiles. They were not scared of them!

"WHY NOT?" asked the
biggest croc of the lot.

"Because we are brave and fearless",
said the three adventurous boys together.

"I have my spear that goes WHOOSH!"
"I have my axe that goes CHOP! CHOP!"
"I have my boomerang that goes WHOOP! WHOOP! WHOOP!"

"THAT'S WHY WE ARE NOT AFRAID OF YOU!"
laughed the boys.

The biggest croc opened wide his huge mouth and showed all his sharp teeth. "OH! REALLY" he roared, "Let's see how brave you really are!"

The biggest croc in the billabong lunged out of the water and his jaws went SNAP! SNAP! "AAHH! AAHH! AAHH!" screamed the boys as they ran away.

The End

Suggestions on ways to have more fun using this book

Counting to three:

There are three boys, three 'toys', three didgeridoos and three crocodiles. One to one correspondence: Each boy has a 'toy'. Each one has a didgeridoo and a crocodile that might eat them up.

Word Awareness:

The lovely sounds of whoosh, chop, whoop and woom woomma get little mouths working. This is an interesting way for young children to become aware of the connection between sounds and the printed word. Accompanying hand actions: Children can pretend to throw the spear and make the whoosh sound, pretend to chop with the axe and whirl their hands to whoop when throwing the boomerang. They can also be encouraged to cup their hands to their mouths and blow through them to make the wonderful woom woomma sound of the didgeridoo. It's noisy!

Looking at Culture:

The 'toys' in the book can be a conversation starter with children about the First Peoples of Australia and the tools that were used and are still in use today. There can be discussion on how the boys came by their 'toys'. How the spear was made, the boomerang was a community effort between a child and his father and the boomerang was handed down from a grandad. This explores resourcefulness and independence (spear), getting help from your community (axe) and the specialness of having a heirloom passed down to you from an Elder (boomerang). This discussion can be extended into cultures and ways of life. A follow up story that explores looking at beginning the journey of reconciliation is *Sorry Sorry* by the Anne Kerr also published by Boolarong Press.

Safety:

The boys are full of bravado. Should they be concerned about the crocodiles? Did they see the snake or the warning sign on the way to the billabong? These questions could begin a discussion about appropriate risk taking and how children can keep themselves and their friends safe in their own environments ie. road safety, water safety.

This is a book for those with adventurous spirits. Have fun.

Anne Kerr